THE LOCKHORNS

by Bill Hoest

TOR

A TOM DOHERTY ASSOCIATES BOOK
NEW YORK

THE LOCKHORNS: LEROY IS VERY PROUD

Copyright © 1969, 1970, 1971, 1974, 1975, 1984, 1989 by King Features Syndicate, Inc.

A TOR Book
Published by Tom Doherty Associates, Inc.
49 West 24 Street
New York, NY 10010

ISBN: 0-812-50601-4   Can. ISBN: 0-812-50602-2

First edition: December 1989

Printed in the United States of America

0 9 8 7 6 5 4 3 2 1

"I WOULDN'T SAY HE DIDN'T NOTICE IT.......
HE ASKED ME WHAT DIED."

'JUST A MINUTE..... HE'S BUSY
ELECTROCUTING THE TOAST."

"HE WANTS TO KNOW IF WE HAVE ANY
ANNIVERSARY CARDS EDGED IN BLACK."

"GOOD LUCK."

"I JUST DONT KNOW WHAT WE COULD ELIMINATE TO BALANCE THE BUDGET!"

"I GUESS THAT'S ABOUT ALL THEY TOOK···· OH, YES······MY WIFE IS MISSING, TOO."

"I KNOW I SHOULD HAVE A GOOD BREAKFAST...
BUT LORETTA ALWAYS GETS
UP IN TIME TO FIX MINE."

"YOU'RE LEAVING THIS HOUSE OVER MY
DEAD BODY!"

4-1

"WHAT DO YOU MEAN, I WAS FOLLOWING TOO CLOSE? YOU WEREN'T KEEPING FAR ENOUGH AHEAD!"

"LETTER FROM MOTHER?"

"EXCUSE ME......YOUR WIFE'S ON THE PHONE, SWEETIE!"

"IT'S A RECORDED LETTER FROM YOUR MOTHER........ON AN L.P."

"THERE'S A LOT TO BE SAID ABOUT MARRIAGE......
LORETTA IS STILL SAYING IT EVERY
MORNING AT BREAKFAST."

4-5

5-22

"BUT YOU TOLD ME TO CLEAN THE FISH!"

HoEST
4-14

"LORETTA HAS A FANTASTIC MEMORY! ONLY YESTERDAY SHE REMEMBERED SOMETHING THAT HAPPENED WAY BACK WHEN SHE WAS THIRTY-NINE!"

HoEST
7-11

"YES, SHE'S HERE.... WOULD YOU LIKE TO LISTEN TO HER?"

"MY MOTHER CAN EVEN THAW A BETTER DINNER THAN YOU CAN!"

"HE WAS PERFECTLY TAME UNTIL HE TASTED YOUR POTATO SALAD."

"IDIOT!"

"HE HATES EVERYONE, REGARDLESS OF
RACE, CREED OR COLOR."

5-1

12-19

"HE'S EXHAUSTED. THIS MORNING HIS
ELECTRIC TOOTHBRUSH BURNED OUT
AND HE HAD TO FINISH THE JOB BY HAND."

"MA'AM, THAT **WAS** IN LAYMAN'S LANGUAGE!"

"EVEN IF I WERE A MOTH
I WOULDN'T LIKE IT!"

"THERE'S ONE NICE THING ABOUT
BEING BALD······ IT'S NEAT."

"IT DOESN'T TAKE MUCH TO GET LEROY MAD...
AS LITTLE AS THIRTY-NINE, NINETY-FIVE."

"THE ONLY MAN I KNOW WHO USES THE REMOTE CONTROL TO TURN ON THE EXERCISE PROGRAM."

"I'M SORRY, MRS. LOCKHORN. THERE'S NO ONE HERE WHO FITS THAT DESCRIPTION."

"TELL ME, THE TRUTH, LEROY.
YOU DON'T REALLY LIKE MY
QUICHE LORRAINE!"

"I HAVE TEN DOLLARS····· YES OR NO?"

"I DON'T MIND TAKING LORETTA OUT FOR SUPPER OFTEN.....I'M PROBABLY INCREASING MY LIFE EXPECTANCY!"

"YOU CAN OPEN YOUR EYES NOW.... IT'S STOPPED GROANING."

12-15

"NO, I DIDN'T PUT TOO MUCH SUGAR IN YOUR COFFEE. YOU'RE DRINKING THE PANCAKE SYRUP."

TUNNEL OF LOVE

12-24

"SEPARATE BOATS, PLEASE."

Hoest
1-26

"YES, THE ENGINE IS FLOODED AND NO,
WE DON'T HAVE TO CALL A PLUMBER!"

DINNER
IN
FREEZER

Hoest
5-9

"WHAT'S SHE GOT THAT I HAVENT HAD LONGER?"

NOW PLAYING—
PASSPORT TO MURDER
A CHILLER

"I STOOD UP TO APPLAUD HIS ACTING ABILITY.....NOT BECAUSE HE WAS STRANGLING HIS WIFE."

"WAIT A MINUTE. I JUST HAD A NAP....
LET ME REST AWHILE."

"I'M AFRAID LEROY IS
LOSING HIS WILL TO LEAVE."

"NONSENSE, YOU HAVE A LOT TO LIVE FOR! MY SOCKS NEED DARNING, A BUTTON'S OFF MY SHIRT, THE SINKS FULL OF DIRTY DISHES...."

"WHY CAN'T YOU BE LIKE OTHER HUSBANDS AND SNEAK OUT NIGHTS?"

12-20

"WOULD YOU LIKE TO MUMBLE SOMETHING TO MOTHER?"

12-30

"FOR SUPPER TONIGHT WOULD YOU LIKE A VEAL CUTLET, SPARE-RIBS, SIRLOIN STEAK...

... OR WOULD YOU PREFER TO STAY HOME AND HAVE A PEANUT-BUTTER SANDWICH?"

"I'M SORRY I DIDN'T NOTICE YOU GOT YOUR HAIR FIXED. I DIDN'T EVEN KNOW IT WAS BROKEN."

"NO, THANKS. I HAD A PIECE OF WEDDING CAKE TWENTY-SIX YEARS AGO AND I STILL HAVE INDIGESTION."

"NOW THAT HE HAS SOLVED ALL OUR PROBLEMS WE SHOULDN'T HAVE TO GO BACK UNTIL NEXT WEEK."

"THE DOCTOR'S BILL IS FOR THE MECHANIC WHO WAS STILL UNDER THE CAR WHEN I DROVE IT OUT OF THE SHOP."

"WE'RE INVITED OUT TO DINNER? I HOPE IT'S SOMEWHERE THEY HAVEN'T SEEN MY TWO DRESSES."

Hoest 7-26

"IT'S LEROY'S BIRTHDAY. I'D LIKE THIS CLEANED AND PRESSED AND GIFT-WRAPPED.

Hoest 6-26

"I KNOW YOU'RE LISTENING. I CAN HEAR YOU GRINDING YOUR TEETH!"

"NOTICE EVERY TIME THEY HAVE A BATTLE OF WITS IT ENDS IN A SCORELESS TIE?"

"LISTEN, LEROY! I'VE BALANCED THE BUDGET!
TOMORROW YOU SELL THE CAR, GIVE UP
BOWLING, AND START ON A DIET."

"AND THEN ONE DAY LORETTA'S INCESSANT
CHATTER ACTUALLY STARTED MAKING SENSE!"

12-12

"HONEST, LEROY! I WAS JUST GOING OUT TO
MAIL A LETTER, I DON'T HAVE A SINGLE
CHARGE PLATE ON ME!"

12-13

"WILL YOU EXCUSE MY HUSBAND?
HE'S GOING TO HAVE A HEADACHE."

"LEROY, WOULD YOU MIND IF I VISITED MY SISTER FOR A FEW WEEKS?"

"THIS ISN'T THE ARMY. YOU <u>CAN'T</u> GET A TRANSFER. NOW GET MY SUPPER!"

"THE FAMILY TREE ON LORETTA'S
SIDE IS POISON OAK."

"HERE. WHY DON'T YOU WEAR THIS SERAPE
AND GO AS A MEXICAN HAIRLESS?"

6-27

"I WANT TO RETURN IT. HE DIDN'T SAY 'WOW' LIKE YOU SAID ···· HE SAID, 'OH NO!'"

5-19

"AND THIS IS THE LAB WHERE LORETTA EXPERIMENTS WITH THE FOOD."

"YOU'LL JUST HAVE TO TAKE MY WORD AGAINST A THOUSAND OF HERS."

"DO YOU HAVE ANY <u>TALK</u> SUPPRESSANTS?"

"I'M A GOOD COOK!........
YOU'RE A LOUSY EATER!"

"IMAGINE HIM REMEMBERING YOU AFTER
ALL THOSE YEARS!"

"SURE, YOU WERE THE LIFE OF THE PARTY.
THAT'S WHY IT BROKE UP AT EIGHT-THIRTY."

2-17

"IT KEEPS ME WARM ALL WINTER AND LEROY
HOT AS BLAZES WHEN THE PAYMENTS ARE DUE."

1-1

"I JUST FIGURED OUT THAT ON THE MOON
I'D ONLY WEIGH TWENTY-SEVEN POUNDS!"

Hoest
1-31

"IT BEATS ME HOW ANYONE WITH A
SHAPE LIKE A POTBELLIED STOVE
COULD BE SO COLD."

Hoest
4-25

"LORETTA WON IT FOR BEING CUSTOMER
OF THE YEAR AT ARNIE'S AUTO BODY SHOP!"

"THESE EGGS ARE FRESH FROM THE COUNTRY, EH?......WHAT COUNTRY?"

"DON'T PUT ON AN ACT WITH ME, LORETTA, THE TV IS STILL WARM!"

4-22

"IN THE SPRING AN OLD MANS FANCY TURNS
TO THE SAME THOUGHTS HE HAD
IN WINTER, FALL AND SUMMER."

12-11

"IF I HAD WANTED OVERCOOKED, TASTELESS
FOOD, I WOULD HAVE STAYED HOME!"

"LET'S SEE .....I HAVE A RESERVATION FOR
MR. LOCKHORN AND LARGE PARTY...."

"I CALL THESE MY GOLFING SOCKS
BECAUSE THERE'S A HOLE IN ONE."

"THE WAY I HEARD IT, HE SHOT HIS WIFE
DURING A PERIOD OF TEMPORARY SANITY."

"FEEL LIKE TAKING A LITTLE SWIM, LORETTA?
I FORGOT THE BEER."

"OH, I HUNG UP LONG AGO. I'M JUST
FINISHING MY DOODLE."

"I REALLY THINK WE SHOULD BUY IT, LEROY.
THEN IF WE NEED IT WE'LL HAVE IT."

"I'LL HAVE THE USUAL......
THE UNUSUAL, I GET AT HOME."

7-30
Hoest

"IT'S AMAZING WHEN YOU THINK OF IT, OUR
OAK TREE HAS THE SAME CIRCUMFERENCE
AND IT'S OVER SIXTY FEET HIGH."

Hoest
6-25

"WHAT ARE YOU UP TO <u>NOW</u>, LORETTA?"

"CAN'T YOU HURRY UP THOSE
THREE-MINUTE EGGS?"

"YES, I'M TAKING IT BACK. LEROY LIKED IT AND YOU KNOW WHAT POOR TASTE HE HAS."

"I'M ALL ALONE AT THE MOMENT, MURRAY. MY MOTHER-IN-LAW RECALLED MY WIFE!"

7-1

"I NOTICE YOU TOOK THE LONG SCENIC ROUTE."

6-28

"I WOULD USE SOME OF MY WILL POWER TO KEEP
FROM EATING, BUT I'M USING ALL MY WILL
POWER TO KEEP FROM BUYING A NEW HAT."

7-4 Hoest

"LORETTA, CAN'T YOU MOW FASTER?
I'M HUNGRY!"

7-8 Hoest

"LORETTA HAS A CHRONIC NOSE PROBLEM....
IT KEEPS POKING INTO PEOPLE'S BUSINESS."

"EVERY MEAL'S THE SAME····ONE CANNED THING AFTER ANOTHER!"

"THERE WAS A TIME WHEN I WORSHIPPED LEROY FROM AFAR. WHY, OH, WHY, COULDN'T I LEAVE IT THAT WAY?"

"IT'S ONLY JULY AND ALREADY SHE'S NAGGING
ME TO TAKE DOWN THE STORM WINDOWS."

"I WOULDN'T KISS ANYBODY'S WIFE
IN A GETUP LIKE THAT!"

"I DON'T LIKE THE WAY SHE LOOKS, EITHER, BUT TRY TO SAVE HER......HER COOKING REALLY ISN'T HALF BAD."

"IN CASE WE NEVER SEE EACH OTHER AGAIN I'LL SAY GOOD-BYE RIGHT NOW."

"QUICK! THE LIBRARY.....IT'S SOUNDPROOFED!"

"I LIKE IT........IT'S GARBAGE, BUT I LIKE IT."

"MY MOUTH KEEPS SNAPPING SHUT.
I SUPPOSE IT'S NATURE'S WAY OF PROTECTING
ME FROM YOUR TUNA CASSEROLE."

CRUISE TO TAHITI

TAKE YOUR
WIFE ALONG

"IT'S LIKE TAKING A SANDWICH
TO A BANQUET."

"I'VE GOT AN IDEA. THIS MORNING.
YOU SET THE TABLE AND I'LL
BURN THE BACON."

7-3

7-4

"THIS WOULDN'T HAVE HAPPENED IF YOU'D
HAD THEM CHECK THE OIL AS I ASKED YOU TO."

"LEROY, I JUST BACKED THE CAR OVER THE LAWN MOWER."

"OF COURSE I DON'T BELIEVE IN THIS ASTROLOGY NONSENSE. WE VIRGOS AREN'T EASILY TAKEN IN."

"THE MAILMAN BROUGHT A PACKAGE FROM YOUR MOTHER. IT'S IN THE KITCHEN SINK UNDER WATER."

"ER........CAN YOU GIFT-WRAP IT, PLEASE?"

"YOU WANT TO FIND OUT WHAT YOUR GIRL FRIEND REALLY THINKS OF YOU?....... MARRY HER!"

"DID YOU HAVE TO DO ALL THE CLEARING YOURSELF?"

6-5

"THIS RECIPE HANDED DOWN BY YOUR
SWEDISH GRANDMOTHER SEEMS TO
HAVE SUFFERED IN THE TRANSLATION."

"WELL, YOU CAN'T HAVE A DIVORCE FOR YOUR
BIRTHDAY. WHAT ELSE DO YOU WANT?"

"A LITTLE MORE TO THE LEFT·····
A LITTLE MORE·····NOW·····STRAIGHT DOWN."

"SO I HAVE A DIRTY MIND! I DON'T CHANGE
IT AS OFTEN AS YOU CHANGE YOURS."

"I RAN INTO YOUR OLD FLAME. WE DISCUSSED
YOU AT LENGTH······ AND WIDTH."

"OF COURSE SHE SMILED AT YOU! IT WAS
PROBABLY ALL SHE COULD DO TO KEEP
FROM LAUGHING OUT LOUD!"

"I THOUGHT YOU SAID OUR CREDIT CARD
WAS GOOD ANYWHERE!"

"LEROY USED TO HAVE A THICK HEAD OF HAIR.
NOW HE JUST HAS A THICK HEAD."

"IT'S YOUR DENTIST.
YOUR EXTRA MOUTH IS READY."

"AND YOU SAID IT WOULD BE CHEAPER BY
BUS! SOMEONE STOLE MY PURSE
WITH FIFTY DOLLARS IN IT!"

"WHEN <u>YOU</u> PUT IT ON, THE FRENCH DESIGN LOSES SOMETHING IN THE TRANSLATION."

"IT'S BEAUTIFUL, LEROY.... WHAT DOES IT REPRESENT?"

"THIS IS MY HUSBAND......
HE'S MARRIED!"

"I WAS RIGHT ABOUT THE FUNNY NOISE....
SEE HOW HE'S SMILING!"

"OF COURSE WE'RE HAPPY! SOMETIMES YOU ASK THE STUPIDEST QUESTIONS!"

"IT'S A NOTE TO ME FROM YOUR MOTHER."

"LORETTA IS ONE HUNDRED PER CENT RIGHT...
ABOUT TWO PER CENT OF THE TIME."

"BOY! YOU'LL NEVER BELIEVE <u>THIS</u> ONE.......!"

"IF YOU SAY YOUR WIFE'S A DOG, THEN TRY TO LOOK AT IT THIS WAY..... A DOG IS MAN'S BEST FRIEND!"

"THIS IS THE FIRST TIME THE CANDLES HAVE COST MORE THAN THE CAKE."

"YOU FORGOT MY PIPE TOBACCO!"

6-23

6-29

"YOU DON'T HAVE TO SAY ANYTHING....
YOU _LISTEN_ LIKE AN IDIOT!"

"WELL, YOU SHOULDN'T WEAR THOSE STUPID CURLERS TO BED!"

"LEROY·········???
WHO DID I JUST DRIVE TO THE STATION?"

8-12

"LEROY'S AT THE DENTIST TO HAVE HIS FANGS CLEANED."

8-25

POINT LOOKOUT!

"DO YOU WANT ME TO SMILE OR LOOK NATURAL?"

9-14

"LEROY USED TO BE ALL HEART,
BUT NOW THE STOMACH IS TAKING OVER."

8-13

"MEET MY HANDICAP."

8-11

"WOULD YOU MIND PLAYING SOME OTHER PLACE? MY HUSBAND HAS A HEART CONDITION."

MARRIAGE COUNSELOR

9-15

"EVERY NIGHT WHEN I COME HOME THE PHONE IS HOT AND THE SUPPER IS COLD!"

"LEROY'S IN THE BACKYARD CULTIVATING."

"HERE COMES MR. LOCKHORN......
ONE DOZEN SNAPDRAGONS."

"ANYTHING YOU'D LIKE TO SAY TO MOTHER
THAT WON'T GET YOU IN TROUBLE WITH
THE POSTAL AUTHORITIES?"

"I BUY ANTIQUES. THAT DOESN'T
MEAN I'M A JUNKIE!"

8-24

"EVEN HIS THREATS ARE IDLE."

9-8

"LEROY HAS FOUND A USE FOR MY OLD
DATED DRESSES······HE MAKES ME WEAR THEM."

"WHY DID YOU GIVE ME COFFEE? I TOLD YOU
I WAS SUPPOSED TO AVOID SOLIDS!"

"YOU WANTED TO CUT THE ENTERTAINMENT
BUDGET, DIDN'T YOU?"

"FOR HEAVEN'S SAKE......IF YOU'RE SO AFRAID OF MUGGERS, TAKE YOUR MOTHER ALONG!"

8-17

"EVERYONE HAS A BREAKING POINT. WITH LEROY IT'S ANYTHING OVER TEN DOLLARS."

9-25

"I HATE TO NOURISH GOSSIP, BUT THEN IT'S SUCH A SHAME TO LET IT DIE."

MARRIAGE COUNSELOR

"THE TROUBLE IS, LEROY, YOU DON'T LISTEN AS FAST AS SHE TALKS!"

"OF COURSE THERE'S TWENTY CENTS MISSING
FROM MY PAY ENVELOPE.
I BOUGHT RAQUEL WELCH A HOT DOG."

"HER PAIN IS GONE, DOC. BUT NOW SHE
CAN'T SLEEP WORRYING WHERE IT WENT."

"LEROY'S ON A 'DO IT YOURSELF' KICK. WHEN I ASK HIM TO DO SOMETHING HE SAYS, 'DO IT YOURSELF.' "

"DON'T WORRY IF THE STEAK'S A LITTLE TOUGH. THE COFFEE WILL DISSOLVE IT."

"I FIRST MET LEROY AT A DISCOUNT STORE, WHICH SHOULD TELL YOU SOMETHING."

"TELL YOUR SISTER WE'RE SORRY WE MISSED HER WEDDING, BUT WE'LL BE SURE TO CATCH THE DIVORCE."

"WHAT'S SO STYLISH ABOUT SEE-THROUGH DRESSES? I'VE HAD SEE-THROUGH SOCKS FOR YEARS."

"IT'S TAKEN A LOT OF EFFORT, BUT I'VE FINALLY CONQUERED MY DRIVING AMBITION TO SUCCEED."

"I'VE STUCK WITH LEROY THROUGH THIN AND THICK····FROM 150 TO 195 POUNDS."

"I TOLD HER THAT HER SEAMS WERE CROOKED, AND SHE WASN'T WEARING STOCKINGS."

"IT WAS ONE OF THOSE FREAK ACCIDENTS.....
I ASKED HER TO MARRY ME."

"CHICKEN Á LA KING AGAIN ?"

"OKAY. I'M SORRY I CALLED YOU A BIG GOSSIP.
I DIDN'T KNOW IT WAS SUCH A SECRET."

"ISN'T THERE ANOTHER WAY YOU
CAN GET EVEN WITH ME?"

"I JUST HIT OUR SECOND CAR WITH OUR FIRST CAR."

"WOMEN! WHAT WOULD WE EVER DO WITHOUT THEM?"

"WELL, I PAID MY TRAFFIC TICKET, BUT I GOT ANOTHER ONE ON THE WAY THERE AND ANOTHER ONE ON THE WAY BACK."

"WHAT DO YOU SUPPOSE IS GIVING YOU THESE NIGHTMARES?"

"WHAT DO YOU MEAN YOU'RE GOING TO
REARRANGE THE FURNITURE IN THE BATHROOM?"

"OKAY, LET'S COMPROMISE. IF YOU'LL STOP
TALKING I'LL START LISTENING."

8-10

"EVERY TIME I ASK HIM TO TAKE DOWN THE TREE
HE ACCUSES ME OF NAGGING HIM."

8-27

"THERE WAS ONLY ENOUGH MONEY FOR A
CHEAP VACATION FOR TWO OR A
SWINGING VACATION FOR ONE."

9-7

"YOUR MOTHER WANTS TO KNOW IF WE'LL PICK HER UP AT THE STATION. WHAT SHOULD I TELL HER?"

9-29

"LORETTA'S SHY ABOUT HER AGE....
.... BY ABOUT TWELVE YEARS."

BEST
10-10 ©

"WHAT DO YOU MEAN, MY WIFE IS OUTSPOKEN ?
NOBODY CAN OUTSPEAK LORETTA!"

best
10-22

"HURRY IT UP. MY SUIT'S GETTING DUSTY."

"THERE. THAT SHOULD DRY BY FALL."

"OKAY, I'LL HAVE SECONDS. JUST SO I DON'T
HAVE TO EAT IT TOMORROW."

"RIGHT HERE ON SEPTEMBER TWENTY-THIRD, NINETEEN FIFTY-ONE, YOU SAID I'M BEAUTIFUL WHEN I'M ANGRY!"

"HOW ABOUT LEAVING IN THE TOOTH AND TAKING OUT THE TONGUE?"

"HE HAS AN INFLATED EGO
WITH STOMACH TO MATCH."

"IF YOU WANT TO SAVE FACE, WHY DON'T YOU
KEEP THE BOTTOM PART OF IT SHUT?"

"YOU KNOW VERY WELL WE'RE HAVING DUCK FOR DINNER, LEROY. I'M NOT "COOKING YOUR GOOSE"!"

" I BROUGHT MY LUNCH."

"I DIDN'T SAY I WANTED YOU OUT OF MY LIFE. I SAID I WISHED YOU HAD NEVER COME INTO IT!"

"IT'S YOUR STOCKBROKER AND HE WANTS ME TO BRING YOU A CHAIR."

"JUST WHEN I THINK I CAN MAKE ENDS MEET, SOMEONE MOVES THE OTHER END."

"I TALKED TO YOUR MOTHER SO LONG MY EAR GOT SORE!"

"SINCE WHEN HAVE YOU EVER HAD A
HUMBLE OPINION?"

"PEOPLE SAY WE HAVE A STABLE MARRIAGE
BECAUSE YOU NEVER CLEAN THE HOUSE!"

"WHY IS IT WHEN I BUY SOMETHING
YOU CAN'T EAT OR DRINK
YOU CONSIDER IT AN EXTRAVAGANCE?"

"IT SEEMS THAT TV IS DRIVING US TO
THE MOVIES AND THE MOVIES KEEP
DRIVING US BACK TO TV!"

9-11

"DON'T FORGET TO TAKE YOUR
MOTHER'S PICTURE."

12-23

"I GUESS FIVE DOLLARS WILL HAVE TO
DO. I DON'T HAVE THE TIME OR ENERGY
TO GET ANY MORE OUT OF YOU."

"YOU CAN START GRUMBLING.
BREAKFAST IS READY."

"I'LL SAY THIS FOR YOU. YOU'RE NOT AS
IMPOSSIBLE AS YOU USED TO BE."

"BUT WHAT'S <u>WRONG</u> WITH THE TWENTY PLASTIC GARBAGE-DISPOSAL BAGS I GAVE YOU FOR YOUR BIRTHDAY?"

"OF COURSE I WANT YOU TO HAVE A NOURISHING BREAKFAST. HERE ARE DIRECTIONS TO SAFRAN'S DINER."

"DON'T BE STUPID, OPERATOR. IF I KNEW HER NAME I'D LOOK IT UP MYSELF."

"THAT'S LEROY'S IDEA OF A WELCOME WAGON."

"DO YOU HAVE ANY LIPSTICK THAT CONTAINS GLUE?"

"I CAN'T GO SHOPPING WITH YOU, HARRIET. I'M UNDER HOUSE ARREST"

"WE'VE BEEN ALL THROUGH THIS BEFORE, LEROY.
YOUR MARRIAGE CERTIFICATE DOES <u>NOT</u> HAVE
AN EXPIRATION DATE!"

"WHY, THIS IS DELICIOUS!
DID YOU DISCOVER IT BY MISTAKE?"

"STOP DREAMING, LEROY. YOU'RE TAPERED THE WRONG WAY."

"NO, I DON'T CARE FOR RICE. I ASSOCIATE IT WITH MY BIGGEST MISTAKE!"

11-23

"YOU NEVER LISTEN TO ME!
I TOLD YOU TO PICK UP YOUR FEET!"

"POLISHING THE HORN BUTTON········WHY?"

11-18

"I GET A WARM SPOT IN MY HEART
WHENEVER I THINK OF LORETTA'S COOKING....
IT'S CALLED HEARTBURN."

"WE MAY BE 'MIDDLE CLASS INCOME' BUT
WE'RE CERTAINLY UPPER CLASS OUTGO!"

Hoest 11-27

"I DIDN'T JUST GIVE YOU A DIRTY LOOK.
YOU WERE BORN WITH IT."

Hoest 4-1

"THAT'S RIGHT. LORETTA JUST PASSED ANOTHER
BIRTHDAY·····HEADING IN THE WRONG DIRECTION."

"OF COURSE, I HAD TO DO A LITTLE ARM TWISTING TO GET IT."

"I HAVE SOMETHING I'D LIKE TO DISCUSS WITH YOU IN A CALM, SENSIBLE, OBJECTIVE MANNER, YOU NO GOOD BIRDBRAIN."

3-11

"HOW CAN I ALWAYS 'START THE ARGUMENTS'
WHEN I COMPLETELY IGNORE HER?"

3-18

"LEROY!"

"I KNOW YOU ARE, MOTHER, AND LEROY IS THINKING ABOUT YOU, TOO."

"DO YOU HAVE ANYTHING WITH A VEIL?"

2-27

HOEST

"THAT'S WONDERFUL! NOW THAT THE COMPANY GIVES YOU MORE LEISURE TIME, YOU CAN GET ANOTHER JOB."

Hoest
11-25

"WELL, WE'VE BEEN MARRIED A GOOD NUMBER OF YEARS AND A BAD NUMBER OF YEARS."

"THAT'S LEROY. HE CAN'T BEAR TO
SEE ME WORK."

"I DIDN'T SAY SHE WAS
A GREAT CONVERSATIONALIST.
I SAID SHE HAD A BIG MOUTH."

"I WAS DOING MY BEST TO LOOK ATTENTIVE, BUT MY EYELIDS JUST SLIPPED."

"NOW, DON'T GO STARTING ANY FIGHTS WHEN OTHER MEN PAY ATTENTION TO ME."

"ARE YOU MAKING A DEPOSIT OR WITHDRAWAL?"

"I HEARD YOU SIGH!"

8-29

"POSITIVELY NOT! YOU DON'T HAVE THE
FIGURE FOR IT AND I DON'T
HAVE THE STOMACH FOR IT!"

"YOUR RIGHT TO 'FREE' SPEECH DOESN'T
EXTEND TO THE PHONE COMPANY!"

"NO, I WILL NOT LEND YOU FIVE DOLLARS!"

"IT'S NOT A PEACE SIGN.
I NEED TWO DOLLARS."

11-25

Hoest

"NEED SOME HELP WITH THE DISHES ?"

A328

11-20

Hoest

"JUST BECAUSE I JUST WASHED IT, DON'T
FEEL YOU HAVE TO GO HANG IT UP!"

"OF COURSE I LOVE YOU! DO I HAVE TO
REPEAT MYSELF EVERY YEAR?"

"TRY TO KEEP THE TALK AWAY FROM POLITICS...
WE'RE ALL OUT OF BAND-AIDS."

"I'D BE HAPPY TO GET BACK TO THE POINT WHERE WE WEREN'T SPEAKING TO EACH OTHER."

"YES, I DID SAY SOMETHING, BUT I DON'T REMEMBER WHAT IT WAS······ I DIDN'T KNOW YOU WERE LISTENING."

"WELL, I HEARD YOU REFER TO IT AS 'THIS OLD RAG'!"

"COULDN'T YOU SWITCH THE SUBJECT TO POLITICS OR RELIGION? YOU KNOW HOW YOU ALWAYS WIND UP FIGHTING ABOUT CARS."

"I'M TAKING A TV SURVEY, MA'AM, TO FIND OUT WHAT TV SHOW YOU'RE WATCHING."

1-11

SALVATION ARMY

HOEST
11-1

"IS THIS THE CONCERT YOU'RE TAKING ME TO?"

Hoest
11-28

"DON'T BE DECEIVED BY THE WAY IT LOOKS, GEORGE. ACTUALLY IT'S MUCH WORSE!"

Hoest
11-16

"CERTAINLY I'M INTERESTED IN SAVING OUR MARRIAGE. CAN'T IT WAIT TILL HALF TIME?"

1-12

"OF COURSE HE MOVES SOMETIMES.
WE'VE ONLY BEEN HERE AN HOUR."

10-23

"WE'LL BE HERE AWHILE. SHE HAS A LOT
MORE GOSSIP ABOUT THE
WIDERMANS, THE LENHARTS AND THE WHITES."

"JUST THOUGHT YOU'D LIKE TO KNOW THERE'S A FLOCK OF BIRTHDAY CARDS IN YOUR WIFE'S MAIL THIS MORNING."

"I TOOK YOUR ADVICE AND MADE A LIST OF THE THINGS SHE DOES THAT IRRITATE ME MOST."

"THEY'RE GOING TO AUTOMATE OUR PRODUCTION DEPARTMENT SO ALL WE'LL HAVE TO DO IS PUSH A BUTTON·····YOU KNOW, LIKE A HOUSEWIFE DOES."

"AND HE KEEPS REFERRING TO ME AS, 'HA-HA-THE LITTLE WOMAN.'"